SAN DIEGO PUBLIC LIBRARY

3 1336 02759 8581

S0-CCJ-114

JAN   1992   STORAGE

46%

8581

BB-5

SAN DIEGO PUBLIC LIBRARY

SAN DIEGO PUBLIC LIBRARY
CHILDREN'S ROOM

**ALWAYS BRING YOUR
CARD WITH YOU.**

I Can't Get to Sleep

SIMON & SCHUSTER BOOKS FOR YOUNG READERS
Simon & Schuster Building, Rockefeller Center,
1230 Avenue of the Americas, New York, New York 10020.

Copyright © 1991 by Frank Rodgers
All rights reserved including the right of reproduction in whole or
in part in any form. Originally published in Great Britain by
Conran Octopus Limited. First U.S. edition 1991.
SIMON & SCHUSTER BOOKS FOR YOUNG READERS
is a trademark of Simon & Schuster.
Manufactured in Hong Kong.

10 9 8 7 6 5 4 3 2 1

Library of Congress Cataloging-in-Publication Data
Rodgers, Frank, 1944- I can't get to sleep / Frank Rodgers.
Summary: Bedtime stories told by various family members help
Tom fall asleep but then wake him up again with noisy dreams.
[1. Bedtime—Fiction. 2. Sleep—Fiction. 3. Dreams—Fiction.]
I. Title. PZ7.R6154Iaq 1991 [E]—dc20 90-19607 CP AC
ISBN 0-671-74129-2

FRANK RODGERS

I Can't Get to Sleep

3 1336 02759 8581

SIMON & SCHUSTER BOOKS FOR YOUNG READERS

Published by Simon & Schuster
New York • London • Toronto • Sydney • Tokyo • Singapore

SAN DIEGO PUBLIC LIBRARY
CHILDREN'S ROOM

Tom sat up in bed.

"Mom," he called. "I can't get to sleep."

His mother came in and smiled. "Don't worry, Tom," she said. "You will get to sleep. You just need something nice to dream about. Shall I tell you a story?"

"Once upon a time," she said, "there was an elephant and a rhinoceros who were tired of living in the zoo, so they left and became traveling acrobats. They did backflips, handstands and somersaults in theaters all over the country."

Tom smiled and snuggled down.
"Now go to sleep and dream about them
performing their favorite trick," his mother said,
and kissed Tom goodnight.

But what the elephant and rhino liked doing best
was bouncing up and down on the trampoline.
BOING! BOING! BOING! BOING!

What a noise! It felt as if they were
on the end of Tom's bed.
      Tom sat up again, wide awake.

"I still can't sleep," he called.

So Dad came up the stairs. "I used to dream about pirates when I was little," Dad said. "Lie down and I'll tell you a story about them."

"Once there was a fearsome pirate called Captain Foghorn," Dad said, "who sailed a ship called the *Pretty Polly*."

Tom smiled and closed his eyes.

"The men in his crew were so lazy, they used to leave their cutlasses, wooden legs and treasure lying all over the decks."

Soon Tom was fast asleep and dreaming.

Captain Foghorn was shouting at his crew. "You slovenly seadogs," he roared. "Move yourselves! Dust the mainmast. Iron the sails. Tidy up your

treasure! Then vacuum the deck and polish
the cannon!"

The din was so awful that Tom woke up again.

"I still can't sleep," Tom shouted.

This time Granny came in to see him. "I'll tell you a story," she said. "What would you like to hear about?"

"A rabbit," said Tom. He liked rabbits.

"This is the story of the biggest rabbit in the world," Granny said. "He wanted to play the trumpet

in a band, but no one would have him. He was just too big. Then one day he met two giants. One played the clarinet and the other the guitar, so they formed a trio. Now go to sleep and dream about the lovely music they played," said Granny.

Tom did, but the biggest rabbit in the world and the two giants liked to play Rock 'n' Roll!

BIM BOM BAM! TOOT TOOT, SLAM!

BEEP BEEP BIM BOM TOOT TOOT WHAM!

How could Tom sleep with all that noise going on?

"I can't get to *sleeeep*!" he called out.

Grandpa came in and sat on the bed.

"What can I dream about, Grandpa?" asked Tom.

"I like your bear," said Grandpa. "Why don't you dream about him? Close your eyes and I'll tell you a story."

"Once upon a time a bear had a birthday party. He was five years old. He had a cake with five candles on it and five friends came and gave him five presents. And what do you think they were?"

But Tom was fast asleep and dreaming about the party.

The bears were laughing and dancing and playing games and popping balloons! They made so much noise that Tom woke up again!

"I still can't sleep," Tom said.
"AND IT'S ALL YOUR FAULT!"

"We're very sorry, matey," said Captain Foghorn.
"We didn't know you were so sleepy," said the elephant.
"Why don't we sing you a lullaby?" said his bear.
"What a good idea," said the biggest rabbit in the world.

The band played and they all sang a beautiful lullaby.
The bears sang high sweet notes like choirboys, the
elephant and the rhino sang in the middle and the
pirates sang low down in their boots.

The biggest rabbit in the world and the two giants
played as softly as a whisper.

It was so soothing that everyone fell asleep.

Except Tom and...

"I can't get to sleep," said his bear.

Tom smiled. "You will when you have something nice to dream about," he said. "I will tell you a story."

So he began, "Once upon a time
there was a boy and a bear..."

Then Tom yawned an *enormous* yawn....